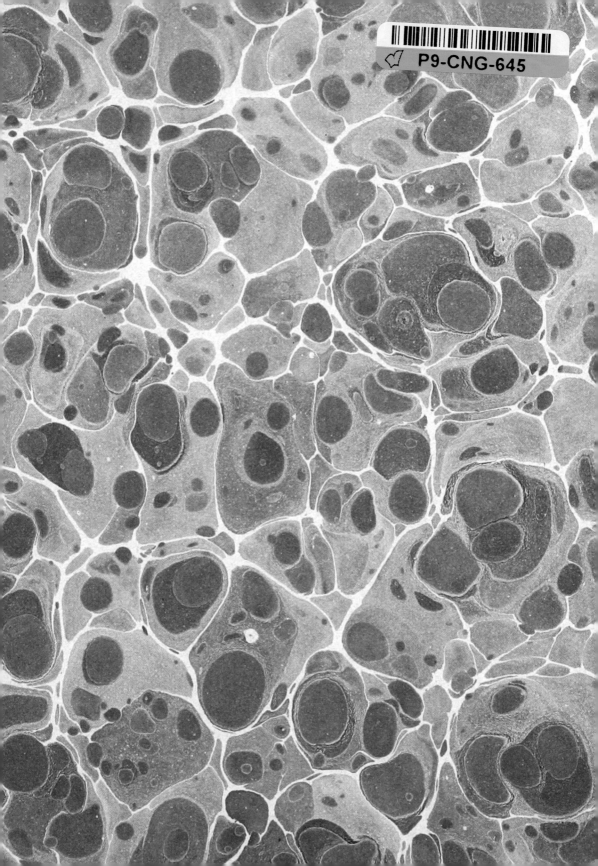

**JOY SORMAN,** a professor of philosophy turned writer, was born in Paris in 1973. She won the prestigious Prix du Flore (2005) for her novel *Boys, Boys, Boys*. She has written numerous books, both for adults and children. *Blob, The Ugliest Animal in the World* marks her US debut.

**OLIVIER TALLEC** is one of France's great illustrators. His work has been described as "sensitive," "stunning," "breathtaking," and "beautiful." Tallec was born in Brittany, France in 1970. Upon graduation from the École Supérieure in Paris, he started to work in advertising as a graphic designer, after which he devoted himself full-time to illustration. Since then, he has illustrated more than seventy books, ten of which have been published by Enchanted Lion.

This work, published as part of a program of aid for publication, received support from the Institut Français. Enchanted Lion Books acknowledges this generous grant with thanks and appreciation.
(Cet ouvrage a bénéficié du soutien des Programmes d'aide à la publication de l'Institut français.)

enchantedlionbooks.com
First published in 2017 by Enchanted Lion Books
67 West Street, Studio 317A, Brooklyn, NY 11222
First published in France in 2015 as *Blob, l'animal le plus laid du monde*
Copyright © 2015 by Actes Sud, France
Copyright © 2017 by Enchanted Lion Books for the English-language translation
All rights reserved under International and Pan-American Copyright Conventions
A CIP record is on file with the Library of Congress
ISBN 978-1-59270-207-7
Printed in China by RR Donnelley Asia Printing Solutions Ltd.
1 3 5 7 9 10 8 6 4 2

Joy Sorman

Illustrated by Olivier Tallec

# BLOB

## THE UGLIEST ANIMAL IN THE WORLD

Translated from the French by Sarah Klinger

ENCHANTED LION BOOKS
NEW YORK

**Blob the Fish** had to travel a very long way to reach us. First, he rose from the depths of the Pacific Ocean, leaving behind the safety of Australia's coastal waters. Next, he boarded a boat, a train, and a plane. To avoid frightening the other passengers, he hid himself inside an overcoat, under a broad brimmed hat.

Every year, Blob has made this difficult journey.
Every year, he has stood before the jury,
hoping to win the famous contest.
But so far, he has come in only second or third.

**The first time Blob entered the contest,** he was upstaged by a frog from Lake Titicaca. The second time, he was beaten by a Kakapo parakeet—a bird so awkward and dumpy it couldn't even fly. The third time, a Sea Pig won gold. And Blob, both proud and sensitive, was outraged at the injustice of it all.

It enraged Blob not to be recognized for his true worth. When a member of the jury called him "more darling and adorable than ugly and repulsive," he felt even worse, and he almost blew his top at the judge's offer to adopt him as a pet. How horrifying! How shameful!

"But this year will be different," thinks Blob. "This year I am going to win."

In the great hall where the world's ugliest animals are welcomed, an expert jury of great scientists and famous artists finally calls Blob to the stage to admire his ugliness.

The introduction is brief: "Some applause, please, for Blob the Fish! Consider his slimy and stunning array of facial features, his sea monster allure, his graceless silhouette, his formidably formless physique, and his sad and sheepish demeanor. So comic! So pitiful!"

"Next, we have the Bald Uakari Monkey, the Naked Mole Rat, the Aye-Aye Lemur, the Star-Nosed Mole, the Proboscis Monkey, the Axolotl, and the Vietnamese Leaf-Nosed Bat!"

The jury retires to deliberate. After what seems like an eternity, Blob the Fish is declared the "Ugliest Animal in the World!"

Thunderous applause erupts. Rose petals and confetti rain down. A young boy approaches Blob with a crown of diamonds, which squeaks quietly against his scaly head.

The president of the Ugly Animal Preservation Society gives a speech in Blob's honor: "Pandas do not have a monopoly on our hearts and kittens have forced their agenda for far too long! Otters are not as sweet as they'd have you believe, koalas are deceitful, and we simply cannot trust baby rabbits! It's time for us to fight back!"

"For ages, these allegedly adorable animals have profited from our attention at the expense of the ugly ones who are punished for their looks. And yet, admire the magnificently soft, gelatinous consistency of Blob the Fish. Blob, we are counting on you to represent the ugly animals of land, sea, and sky with elegance and pride!"

**Thus begins Blob's world tour** as the new ambassador of ugly animals. Received like a king and worshiped as a god, his image is splashed across the cover of numerous magazines.

Before he was named Ugliest Animal in the World, Blob lived 3,000 feet underwater, where his overwhelming ugliness prompted cries of fear and disgust from all the other creatures. But now great designers dress him, famous actresses pose with him, autograph collectors hound him, and fans beg to rub his slimy body for good luck. Cameras flash in his wake.

Naturally, the Queen of England invites him to tea. He hands out prizes to rare cows and pigs at State Fairs. And despite his baldness, Blob becomes the official spokesperson for the annual Global Hairstyling Conference.

Blob attends the International Contemporary Art Fair and poses for a world-class sculptor.

Blob carries the torch at the opening ceremony of the Olympics.

Blob delivers a lengthy speech on climate change at the UN, arguing that it threatens humans as much as the world's ugliest. He talks about the destruction of the seabed, where he makes his home.

It's a life on the road for Blob, with ribbon cuttings, hospital visits, meetings with earthquake victims, fundraising galas, and fashion shows.

**As you might expect,** all of this attention goes straight to Blob's head.

Suddenly, he needs round the clock attention, caviar for breakfast, and of course, a private jet. He fires his makeup artist without provocation and cancels appearances at the last minute. His tantrums are legendary.

As his reign comes to an end and the next contest nears,
Blob grows increasingly despondent, finally descending into
a deep depression.

Who is Blob the Fish?

Since he can't compete again, he'll have to give up
everything—the love, the fame, even his sparkling crown.

**At last, the fateful day arrives.** The stage for this year's Ugliest Animal Contest is assembled. The jury is in place. The numbered bibs are handed out. Before you know it, all eyes are on the Forked-Tail Caterpillar, who is unanimously declared the Ugliest Animal in the World.

Just like that, the spotlight goes out on Blob the Fish.

**All that remains** for Blob is to return home. He boards a plane, a train, and a boat, but this time he goes without his overcoat and hat, hoping someone will recognize him.

Waves pound the sand. Otherwise, it is quiet. Blob sinks 3,000 feet down, back to the ocean floor.

**Like any traveler who returns home,** Blob
has many stories to tell. Sometimes, the bright lights and
sparkling diamonds he describes seem far from beautiful.

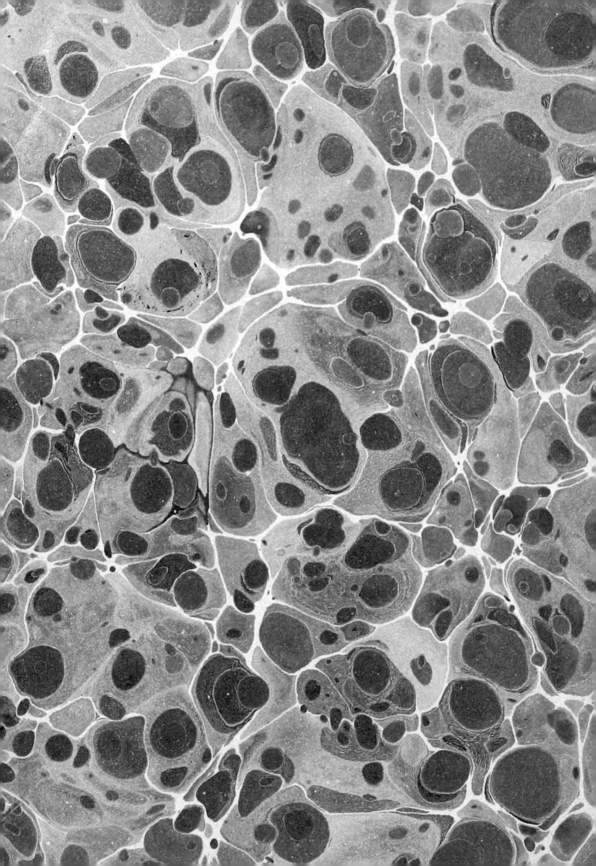